**Read all the books in the
Royal Sweets series!**

## Royal Sweets
### By Helen Perelman

**Welcome to ALADDIN Q**

If you are looking for fast
with colorful characters,
humor, easy-to-follow act
story lines, and lively illu
**ALADDIN QUIX** is for y

But wait, there's more!

If you're also looking for
tables of contents; word l
book questions; 64, 80, o
chapters; short paragrap
then **ALADDIN QUIX** is

**ALADDIN QUIX:** The nex
to reads and longer, more
books, for readers five to ei

# ROYAL SWEETS

## The Marshmallow Ghost

By Helen Perelman

Illustrated by Olivia Chin Mueller

**ALADDIN QUIX**

New York London Toronto Sydney New Delhi

For my mom
—H. P.

This book is a work of fiction. Any references to historical events, real people, or real places are used fictitiously. Other names, characters, places, and events are products of the author's imagination, and any resemblance to actual events or places or persons, living or dead, is entirely coincidental.

ALADDIN QUIX
Simon & Schuster Children's Publishing Division
1230 Avenue of the Americas, New York, New York 10020
First Aladdin QUIX hardcover edition September 2019
Text copyright © 2019 by Helen Perelman
Illustrations copyright © 2019 by Olivia Chin Mueller
Also available in an Aladdin QUIX paperback edition.

For information about special discounts for bulk
purchases, please contact Simon & Schuster Special Sales
at 1-866-506-1949 or business@simonandschuster.com.
The Simon & Schuster Speakers Bureau can bring authors to your live event. For
more information or to book an event contact the Simon & Schuster Speakers Bureau
at 1-866-248-3049 or visit our website at www.simonspeakers.com.
Series designed by Jessica Handelman
Jacket designed by Tiara Iandiorio
Interior designed by Heather Palisi and Jessica Handelman
The illustrations for this book were rendered digitally.
The text of this book was set in Archer Medium.
Manufactured in the United States of America 0819 LAK
2 4 6 8 10 9 7 5 3 1
Library of Congress Control Number 2019931560
ISBN 978-1-4814-9487-8 (hc)
ISBN 978-1-4814-9486-1 (pbk)
ISBN 978-1-4814-9488-5 (eBook)

# Cast of Characters

**Princess Mini:** Royal fairy princess of Candy Kingdom

**Princess Taffy:** Princess Mini's best friend

**Prince Frosting:** One of Princess Mini's cousins from Cake Kingdom

**Princess Cupcake:** Prince Frosting's twin

**Gobo:** Troll living in Sugar Valley

**Princess Lolli:** Princess Mini's mother and ruling fairy princess of Candy Kingdom

**Prince Scoop:** Princess Mini's father

**Chipper:** Princess Taffy's royal unicorn

**Beanie:** Royal chef

# Contents

# 1

## Dragon's Day

I, **Princess Mini**, was one very happy princess. School was over for the day, and the next day was Dragon's Day. Dragon's Day was a holiday in Candy Kingdom to honor the dragons that lived in

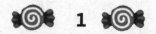

Sugar Valley. There was no school or work for Candy Fairies. I had big plans.

I was planning my first royal sleepover.

My best friend, **Princess Taffy**, was coming. She had been to Candy Castle many times. This would be our first sleepover. We'd already started to make a **schedule** of things to do. We were going to have the best time.

I also asked my cousin **Prince Frosting** to come. Prince Frosting

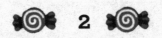

and his twin, **Princess Cupcake**, were my first cousins. They lived in Cake Kingdom.

My parents told me I had to invite Cupcake, too. She was not as sweet as her name sounds. Fortunately, she had other plans for the night.

**Gobo**, my newest friend, was a troll who lived in Chocolate Woods.

For a while, he was my secret friend. Candy Fairies and trolls aren't always friends in Sugar

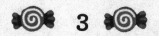 3

Valley. Now things were different.

I was on my way to Chocolate Woods with Taffy and Frosting. Our plan was to ask Gobo to join us at the sleepover.

When we landed in the woods, Gobo was there to greet us.

**"Hello!"** he called. He was holding a large basket of chocolate bark. I love chocolate bark!

"Hi, Gobo," I said. "This looks **choc-o-rific**!"

Frosting reached in the basket

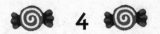

and took a piece. "And they taste
good too!" he said, chewing. Then
Frosting reached for another
piece.

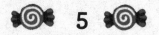

Taffy spread out a blanket on the chocolate sand, and we sat down to have a snack.

"Tomorrow is Dragon's Day," I told Gobo. "We have the day off from school."

**"Sweet!"** Gobo said.

"I'm having a sleepover," I said. "Do you want to come? Taffy and Frosting will be there too."

"We are going to have so much fun," Taffy added.

"A sleepover at Candy Castle?" Gobo asked.

"Yes," Frosting said.

I could see that Gobo was thinking hard. Didn't he want to come?

"Well...," Gobo said. He slowly stood up and walked away.

I looked at Taffy and Frosting. Why was Gobo walking away?

"What's wrong?" I asked. I followed him to the sandy edge of Chocolate River. "I thought you would want to join us."

Taffy and Frosting flew over to us. We stood looking at the milky Chocolate River rushing by.

"This is my first sleepover," Taffy said softly. "I am a little nervous. Are you?"

Gobo turned to Taffy. "Are you scared of the Marshmallow Ghost?" he asked.

Taffy raised her eyebrows high. **"Who is the Marshmallow Ghost?"** she asked.

Frosting clapped his hands and said, "I've never heard of him, but

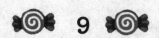

he sounds absolutely **delicious**!"

I rolled my eyes. "There are no ghosts at the castle," I said. "I live there. I should know."

Gobo shifted his feet and looked down. "Well . . . there are stories about a ghost in the tower."

Taffy's dark eyes widened. "Um, didn't you say we were going to sleep in the throne room *in* the tower?" she asked.

"Yes," I said. "The throne room is perfect for a sleepover."

"And perfect for a ghost to visit," Taffy whispered.

"The tower is not **haunted**," I said.

"We'll have fun, Gobo," Frosting said. He stared at Taffy. "Ghosts or no ghosts."

Frosting took another bite of chocolate bark. "I have been to Candy Castle plenty of times, and I have never seen a ghost," he added.

I smiled at Frosting. He could be very nice sometimes.

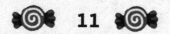

"Sleepovers are full of gooey treats, games, spooky stories, and laughs," I said.

Gobo shrugged. "That does sound like fun," he said.

I flew straight up in the air. "So you will come?" I asked.

"I'll be there," Gobo said. He smiled at me.

**"Sugar-tastic!"** I cheered. "The four of us will have a super-sweet time."

"Let's just hope there isn't room for one more," Taffy said.

"I don't want to meet a ghost in the middle of the night."

I looked at Taffy.

Candy Castle wasn't really haunted . . . was it? Nothing would spoil a royal sleepover more than a ghost.

# 2

## Big Plans

When I got home after being with my friends at Chocolate River, I found my parents in the royal parlor in Candy Castle. They were both reading books.

"Gobo is coming to my sleep-

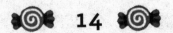

over!" I announced as I flew into the room.

"I am so glad," my mother said. She was **Princess Lolli**, the ruling fairy princess of Candy Kingdom. She really liked Gobo.

"What are the big plans?" my

father asked. He was **Prince Scoop**. He put his book down on his lap.

I took out a list from my bag, and said, "We are going to play games, eat sweets, tell spooky stories . . ." I paused. "And stay up all night!"

"Well, I am not sure about the staying up all night part," my mom said, smiling.

"Have you ever heard of the Marshmallow Ghost?" I asked. "Gobo said he heard stories about a ghost in the castle tower."

"No," my dad said. "But I do like marshmallows." He licked his lips and laughed.

**"Not funny,"** I said. "Taffy is worried. I don't want anyone to be scared at the sleepover."

"I don't think you should worry," my dad said.

"You are going to have a **sweet-tacular** time with your friends," my mom added.

I hoped my parents were right.

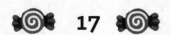

"I am going to look for my friends," I said. "They should be here soon."

I flew to the top of the royal tower. I searched the skies. Finally, I saw **Chipper**, Taffy's unicorn.

Taffy and Gobo were on Chipper's back. I waved and flew down to the gardens where Chipper landed. Frosting arrived at the same time. **Now the party could start!**

I took my friends inside the tower and showed them the throne room.

The room was round and wide. We spread out our sleeping bags.

"This place doesn't look haunted," Frosting said. The large room was full of brightly

colored **tapestries** and rugs made of soft cotton candy.

"Wait until later," Taffy muttered.

We went out into the Grand Hall. Frosting and Gobo raced ahead. Taffy pulled me aside.

"I love stories. I love books," Taffy said. "I am *not* a fan of spooky stories."

"They are just stories," I replied. **"It's fun!"**

"I don't think it is so fun," she said.

Taffy looked over at Gobo and Frosting. She lowered her voice. "What will they say about Bunny?"

Taffy had a stuffed blue bunny with **floppy** ears. She had to sleep with her. I could tell she was

nervous to show Frosting and Gobo her bunny.

"I don't think they will say anything," I told her. "I am going to sleep with Lick, my stuffed unicorn."

"But Lick is *so* small," Taffy said. "You can hide him in your sleeping bag and no one will see. Bunny is big. They will definitely see her."

She was right, but I didn't think it would be a big deal. "Come on," I said. I wanted to change the

subject. "Let's go join their game."

Frosting and Gobo were racing around the large licorice statues in the Grand Hall. My friends were giggling and having fun.

I hoped the rest of the night would be the same.

# 3

## Chocolate Flowers

My friends and I returned to the throne room. Gobo ran the fastest and was the first one back.

"This is fun," Gobo said. He stopped and took some deep breaths. "Do these tell a story?"

He pointed to the large tapestries hanging on the walls.

"Yes," I said. "These tell the **history** of Sugar Valley. They are art, but also a history lesson."

**"There is a troll!"** Gobo said, pointing.

On one of the first wall hangings, there was a small troll.

"He looks like you!" Taffy said. "Maybe he is a royal relative!"

We giggled and sat down on our sleeping bags.

"I have never slept out of Chocolate Woods," Gobo said.

"I am really happy you are here," I told Gobo.

"We all are!" Taffy exclaimed.

"Let's go visit **Beanie**," I said. I turned to Gobo. "She's the royal chef."

"And she always has a sweet treat ready," Frosting added.

"That sounds like someone I want to meet!" Gobo said.

We walked down the stairs to the royal kitchen. It smelled **choc-o-rific**, and Gobo smiled from ear to ear.

**"Yum!"** he said. "What's that delicious treat?"

We found Beanie in front of a **marble** table in the kitchen. She was molding tiny chocolate flowers and placing them on a large, round chocolate cake.

"Princess Mini!" she exclaimed. "This chocolate cake was sup-

posed to be a surprise tonight."

"That's okay, Beanie," I said. **"It looks scrumptious!"**

My friends and I sat around the table.

"Would you like to help?" Beanie asked. She gave us each a piece of chocolate and showed us how to roll the pieces into tiny flowers.

Taffy placed her flower on the cake and then turned to Beanie and asked, "Have you heard of the Marshmallow Ghost in the tower?"

"No," Beanie said. "And I have been the cook here for a long, long time."

I nibbled on a piece of chocolate from the table. "We are going to tell spooky stories later," I said.

Frosting picked up his chocolate flower and was about to put it in his mouth.

**"Hold on!"** Beanie said, stopping Frosting. "Don't eat the decorations yet." She took Frosting's flower.

"I wish I were a ghost," Frosting

said. "Then I could be **invisible**, and you wouldn't know I took the chocolate!"

Beanie laughed. "I would catch you," she said.

"Not if you couldn't see me," Frosting said. "Or if I were super fast!" He quickly took one of the chocolate flowers and popped it in his mouth. "And like a ghost, I will be gone!"

Frosting flew out of the kitchen before Beanie could scold him. **"Thank you, Beanie!"**

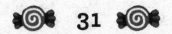

I called as we followed Frosting.

"Don't stay up too late!" Beanie said. "And be careful!"

"Oh, why did she say that?" Taffy asked with a worried look. "There must be ghosts around here," she whispered.

I looked down the long hallway back to the tower. I hoped she was wrong!

# 4

## Sweet Snacks

The sky was dark, and the moon and stars were shining. My parents flew into the throne room.

**"Good evening!"** my dad called.

"Good evening, Princess Lolli

and Prince Scoop," Taffy, Gobo, and Frosting said at the same time.

"This looks very cozy," my mom said, looking around.

We had rolled out our sleeping bags and put extra blankets and pillows around. I smiled. So far, my sleepover was a royal success.

My parents were holding large trays. I flew over to see what they had brought us.

**"Sugar-tastic!"** I said when

I saw the treats. There was Beanie's chocolate cake and a tray of candy jewels.

"Beanie is **choc-o-rific**!" Frosting said. He hovered over the trays, licking his lips.

"She wanted to make sweet treats for you," my mom said. "Here, taste one."

She lowered the tray so Gobo could take one of the chocolates decorated with colored sugar crystals.

"This is the prettiest candy

I have ever seen," Gobo said. He held up the chocolate and **admired** the treat.

"And it will be the tastiest," Taffy told him. "Beanie is a chocolate artist!"

**"Ooooooh,"** Gobo said after

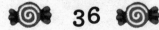

he took a bite. "This is royally good!"

Frosting nodded his head enthusiastically. "Best looking candy *and* best tasting!" He popped the whole candy in his mouth. Then he took a piece of cake and sat down to eat.

I looked at my list. "After our nighttime snack, we are going to tell spooky stories," I said.

**"Spooky stories?"** Taffy asked. Her eyes were wide and her eyebrows high. "I thought we weren't going to do that."

"Are you going to tell us about the Marshmallow Ghost?" Gobo asked my dad.

"No," my dad said. "I don't know about any Marshmallow Ghost."

My mom looked right at Taffy. "There is no Marshmallow Ghost here," she said. Then she turned to Gobo. "Spooky stories are supposed to be for fun scares."

"Let's make up a spooky story about a ghost," Frosting said. "A ghost that eats treats like these!" He reached over to my dad's tray and took another piece of chocolate cake.

I looked at Taffy and Gobo. I didn't think they were so happy about that idea.

"Good spooky stories are meant to make you laugh," my dad said.

"Just like the ghost jokes," I said. "Do you know about the Chocolate Ghost?"

**"Th-there is a Chocolate Ghost?"** Taffy stammered.

"Yes," I said. "He made cookies and *I scream!*"

Gobo giggled. **"Good one, Mini!"**

"What kind of mistakes do ghosts make?" Frosting asked. He started laughing before we could answer. "Boo-boos!!!" he answered, slapping his knee.

I saw Taffy and Gobo laugh.

I loved that my friends were laughing.

"All right, no ghosts here!" my dad said.

"Yes, spooky tales should be fun, not frightening," my mother said. She blew a kiss. "You are safe. Don't stay up too late."

My parents flew out of the room.

I looked at Taffy. I hoped this

made her feel better. "You see?" I said.

"Parents always say things like that," Taffy muttered. She reached out to touch Bunny's floppy ears. Then she grabbed the ears and stuffed him into her sleeping bag.

"Maybe we should **stargaze**?" I suggested.

**"Fun!"** Gobo exclaimed. He dashed out onto the terrace.

"There could be ghosts out here, too," Frosting said.

I shot Frosting a look.

Gobo **scurried** back inside the room.

"What?" Frosting asked. "I'm just saying that there might be ghosts here."

Taffy crawled into her sleeping bag. "I am going to stay here," she said. "You can go if you want."

Gobo slipped into his sleeping bag. "I will stay with you," he said.

Frosting shrugged. "I guess we'll all stay here," he said. "At least there is chocolate."

# 5

## Night Noises

The throne room was dark and quiet.

"Is anyone else up?" Frosting whispered.

"I am," I said.

"Me too," Gobo said.

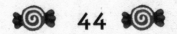

"I'm up. Who can sleep with everyone talking?" Taffy asked.

Frosting snapped on his mint glow stick. He held up the light, and I saw Taffy push Bunny down in her sleeping bag.

**"What is that?"** Frosting asked.

Taffy sat up. "What?"

"What is that blue fur?" Frosting said, moving closer.

Taffy's eyes started to tear up. She didn't want anyone to know about Bunny.

"It looks like this," Gobo said. He pulled out a stuffed dragon with a colorful tail.

"You sleep with him?" Taffy asked.

"Every night," Gobo said. "This is Dee Dee. I have had him since I was a baby."

Frosting sat up. I wasn't sure what he was going to say. Frosting has a sour side and could be mean. I glared at him.

But he did something I didn't **expect**. He pulled out a stuffed bear from his sleeping bag!

"You have a stuffed bear you sleep with?" Taffy asked.

"Yes," Frosting said. "This is Boo!"

**"We all have one!"** I said, laughing. I showed my friends Lick.

"We all have a sleepy friend,"

Taffy said, smiling. She turned to me. "I guess that was something I didn't have to worry about."

**Clang! Clang! Clang!**

"W-w-what was that?" Taffy asked. She hugged Bunny tightly. "Now *that* is something to worry about."

We all froze and looked around the room. No one said a word.

**Cling! Clang! Cling!**

"Frosting!" I scolded. "That isn't funny."

**Cling! Clunk!**

"I didn't do that!" he said, flying out of his sleeping bag.

**"It's the ghost!"** Gobo squealed. He buried his head under his blanket.

"No," I said. "There is no ghost at Candy Castle."

"Then who made those creepy noises?" Taffy asked.

My friends looked very scared. This was going to ruin the sleepover. I had to prove to them that the castle was not haunted.

"Let's go find out," I said. "I am going to prove to you that there is no ghost."

"Are you nuts?" Taffy exclaimed. "I am not going on a ghost hunt!"

I sighed. "There is no ghost," I said.

*Cling! Clang!*

"Are you sure?" Gobo asked, looking around the dark room.

I switched on my mint glow stick and showed my friends that the room was empty.

"The noise is coming from over there," Frosting said. He flew to the door.

"Come on," I said to Taffy and Gobo. "Let's stay together."

"Well, now I am not staying here alone!" Taffy exclaimed.

Gobo moved closer to Taffy. "Me neither," he said.

The hallway was dark. Frosting led the way with his mint **lantern**. I was close behind.

Taffy held my hand.

Gobo held her hand.

"What if we find a Marshmallow Ghost?" Gobo whispered.

No one answered.

"We should go back," Taffy said.

"Come on," I said.

"The sound is coming from the kitchen," Frosting said.

"Do ghosts get hungry?" I asked.

"If I were a ghost," Frosting said, "I would haunt Beanie's kitchen for treats."

**Cling! Clang!**

The four of us jumped.

"We have to go in there," I said.

"We do?" Taffy asked.

I stood straight. My wings

fluttered. "I know there is no ghost," I said. "And I want to prove it to you."

Very slowly, I opened the heavy door.

# 6

## Midnight

**Squeak!**

The old **hinge** on the kitchen
door made a loud sound.

Taffy squeezed my hand tight.

When I pushed open the door,
I saw a bright white light shining

in the middle of the kitchen.

A large lantern was sitting on the table.

**"Prince Scoop?!"** exclaimed Taffy. *"You* are the Marshmallow Ghost?"

My dad laughed. "No, I am not a ghost," he said. "But I am having a midnight snack."

"We thought you were the ghost!" Gobo exclaimed. "All the noises!"

"I am sorry that I was making so much noise," my dad said. "Beanie moved some things around here. I couldn't find what I was looking for in the kitchen."

"Really?" Frosting said. He flew over to my father. "What are you making?" he asked. Then he peered into the large pots.

"These are treats from when I was young," my dad told him. "My mom used to make them for me." He picked up a marshmallow pop from one of the trays.

I laughed. "They look like

ghosts," I said. I held up one of the marshmallow pops. **"We should call these snacks Marshmallow Ghosts!"**

"You were talking so much about marshmallows," my dad said. "It got me thinking about these snacks." He handed each of us a pop. "These are my favorite treats."

"I guess there *are* Marshmallow Ghosts here at Candy Castle," Taffy said, smiling.

"An excellent find!" Frosting

exclaimed. He took a bite and smiled. "These are royally good!"

Gobo took a bite of his marsh-mallow pop. **"Yum,"** he said. "Thank you!"

I was so happy my friends were not scared anymore. And I was very happy to know my castle wasn't haunted.

Taffy started to laugh.

"What is so funny?" I asked.

"We were so scared," she said. "We thought those noises were because there was a ghost, and it was just pots and pans clanging."

We all laughed.

"Did you see Frosting's face?" Taffy asked.

"What about your face?" Frosting said, pointing to Taffy.

"I didn't think my heart could

beat that fast!" Taffy replied.

"We were all scared," Gobo chimed in. "And now that it's over, it was sort of fun!"

I looked over at Taffy. She was smiling.

"It was fun being scared together," Taffy said. "And the best part was that the scare was just Prince Scoop, not a ghost!"

I exclaimed happily, **"Sure as sugar!"**

We sat around the kitchen table and ate the sweet treats.

"Beanie is not going to be happy with this mess," I said. There were bags of sugar and a couple of pots out on the stove. "We should clean up."

"Thank you," my dad said. "I was thinking the same thing. I appreciate you all helping. Marshmallow Ghosts are tasty and messy."

We helped my dad wash and put away the pots. When the kitchen was clean, I sighed. "Beanie will be happy now," I said.

"And that means she will

make us a yummy breakfast," Frosting said, grinning. "Maybe she will make some pancakes and *BOO*-berries," he added.

**"That sounds scary good!"** Gobo giggled.

My dad smiled. "Very funny, but now it is time for sleep."

We went back to the throne room and snuggled up in our sleeping bags.

"Good night, everyone," I said.

"This was the best sleepover ever," Taffy whispered.

I gave Lick a hug. "Yes," I said. "Sleepovers are always fun with friends and marshmallows!"

"And no ghosts!" Gobo added.

I agreed.

I was very happy that there were no ghosts at Candy Castle!

# Word List

**admired (add·MY·urd):** Looked at with great respect

**delicious (dee·LI·shus):** Having very good taste

**expect (ek·SPEKT):** To think that something will probably happen

**floppy (FLAH·pee):** Hanging in a loose way

**haunted (HAWN·ted):** Having ghosts in a place

**hinge (HINJ):** The part of a door that allows it to swing open and closed

**history (HISS·tor·ee):** The story of past events

**invisible (in·VIS·a·bull):** Impossible to see

**lantern (LAN·turn):** A lamp that can be carried

**marble (MAR·bull):** A kind of stone

**schedule (SKEH·jool):** A list of times for things to be done

**scurried (SKUR·reed):** Moved quickly and with short steps

**stargaze (STAHR·gayz):** To look at or study stars in the sky

**tapestries (TAP·ess·trees):** Heavy cloths that have pictures woven into them and are used for wall hangings

# Questions

1. Why doesn't Gobo want to go to the sleepover?

2. What is Taffy afraid of at the start of the sleepover?

3. Do you know a joke about a ghost?

4. Who did you think was making the noises?

5. Do you have a sleepy friend or stuffed animal?

# QUIX FAST·FUN·READS

## LOOKING FOR A FAST, FUN READ?
## BE SURE TO MAKE IT ALADDIN QUIX!